When I'm Bigger, Mama Bear

Rachel Bright

Farrar Straus Giroux

New York

Mama Bear is making lunch.
Bella Bear peeks in the pot.
"Let ME stir it, Mama. Pleeeeease?"

"No!" says Mama. "It's too HOT!"

Bella Bear is not impressed.
She goes to chop
some things instead.
"BELLA, STOP!"
shouts Mama Bear.

"Only grown-up bears cut bread!"

Bella wishes she were grown-up.
Sometimes it just isn't *fair*.
"I will stir and chop," says Bella.
"When I'm bigger, Mama Bear."

"Let's stop cooking,"
Mama says.
"We need to pop down
to the shop."

"I will go!" shouts Bella Bear.
"Not on your *own*! No!
Bella . . . STOP!"

So Bella grabs her bike instead.
She's riding down their little street.
"Not so fast!" cries worried Mama . . .
chasing Bella's speeding feet!

"I could ride on TWO wheels, Mama. This bike is TOO SMALL for me!"

"We'll try it *soon*, my little Bella."
"I'll do it, Mama! You will see!"

At the shop they look for butter.
Bella's pushing her *own* cart.

She's filling it with LOTS of things.
Bella Bear is VERY smart!

Bella Bear has spotted COOKIES!
Right up on the highest shelf.

She knows that Mama Bear loves chocolate. She can get the box herself!

Bella starts to climb toward them.

Up and up she wants to go.

Mama turns around and sees her.
"Oh my goodness! Bella . . . NO!"

But Bella's at the top already!
She turns to Mama's worried face.

Suddenly she feels *quite* high.
She's not sure it's all that safe.

Bella's trying not to cry . . .
She doesn't want to move at all.

She tries her hardest not to wobble.
Suddenly she's feeling *Small* . . .

"Don't you worry!" Mama calls
as Bella makes a little yelp.
"Just stay right there and don't you move . . .
I think I know just how to help!"

Then Mama stretches
up on tiptoe.

She's the tallest bear in town! She wraps her paws round little Bella, scoops her up . . .

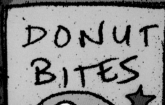

and lifts her down.

Back at home they eat their soup,
dipping in the buttered bread.
Mama smiles at little Bella,
strokes her fur, and pats her head.

"Everyone needs help sometime,
you from me and me from you.
Whenever you might need
a paw . . . well,

I will always help you through."

"You know, my little Bella Bear ...
being bigger CAN be great.
You get to stir and chop and shop,
climb up high and stay up late.

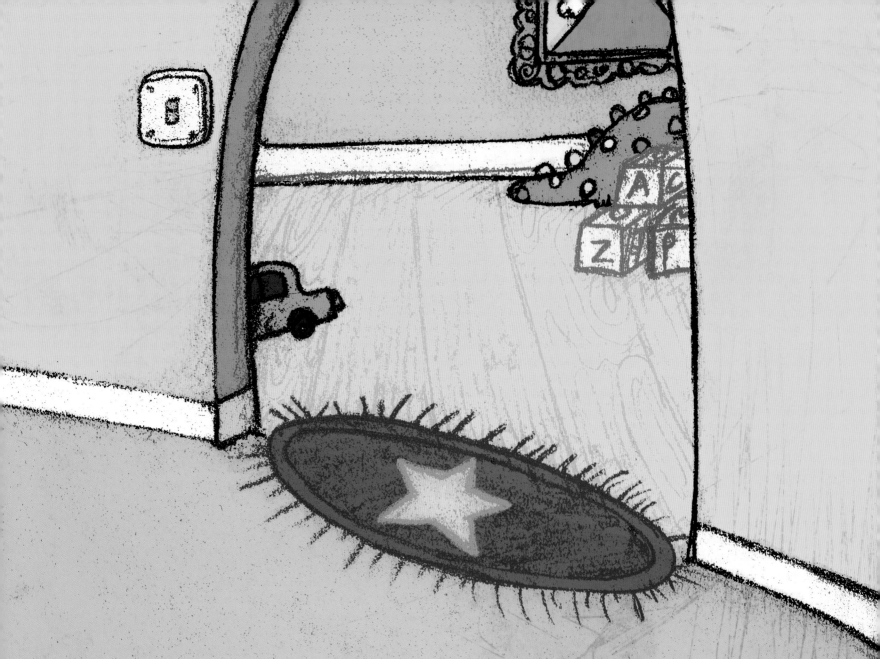

"But when you're small, you're wild and free . . .
you can play without a care.
You *will* understand, my Bella . . ."

"When I'm bigger, Mama Bear."

For River and Sky,
May you always be wild and free.
x R.B.

Farrar Straus Giroux Books for Young Readers
An imprint of Macmillan Publishing Group, LLC
120 Broadway, New York, NY 10271
Copyright © 2020 by Rachel Bright
All rights reserved
Color separations by Bright Arts (H.K.) Ltd.
Printed in China by RR Donnelley Asia Printing Solutions Ltd.,
Dongguan City, Guangdong Province
Designed by Monique Sterling
First edition, 2020

1 3 5 7 9 10 8 6 4 2

mackids.com

Library of Congress Cataloging-in-Publication Data
Names: Bright, Rachel, author, illustrator.
Title: When I'm bigger, Mama Bear / Rachel Bright.
Other titles: When I am bigger, Mama Bear
Description: First edition. | New York: Farrar Straus Giroux, 2020. | Audience: Ages 2–6. | Audience: Grades K–1. |
Summary: Bella is so eager to help Mama Bear with cooking and shopping that she forgets her size.
Identifiers: LCCN 2020007737 | ISBN 9780374305802 (hardcover)
Subjects: CYAC: Stories in rhyme. | Mothers and daughters—Fiction. | Bears—Fiction. | Size—Fiction.
Classification: LCC PZ8.3.B7678 Wh 2020 | DDC [E]—dc23
LC record available at https://lccn.loc.gov/2020007737

Our books may be purchased in bulk for promotional, educational, or business use. Please
contact your local bookseller or the Macmillan Corporate and Premium Sales Department at
(800) 221-7945 ext. 5442 or by email at MacmillanSpecialMarkets@macmillan.com.